Memoirs

...of her past loves

Memoirs

...of her past loves

Sapphire

Memoirs of Her Past Loves

Book Cover Design by Sharhonda Dunlap

ISBN: 978-1-7355315-2-6 (paperback)

First Edition: January 2021

10 9 8 7 6 5 4 3 2 1

Coming Soon by Sapphire

The Man She Never Had

We're Both a Secret

Books by Sapphire

The Woman She Became – Part I

The Woman She Became – Part II

Memoirs of Her Past Loves

Memoirs of Her Past Loves

Memoirs

...of her past loves

Sapphire

"LOVE needs to make sense! Be genuine, not pretentious to grab my attention and I will aim to make myself invaluable to you."

Contents

Section One
The Forbidden One
Pages 1-26

Section Two
The "First" True Love
Pages 27-62

Section Three
The Lost One
Pages 63-70

Section Four
The Extras
Pages 71-81

Memoirs of Her Past Loves

Dedication

To all of my past loves, thank you for the experiences!

To my future, I welcome you with an extremely delicate, but open heart and an open mind. I look forward to what you have in store for me.

Dear My True Love,

You are a part of my being. You mixed with my thoughts, even the most studious, and instead of disturbing them, you give them greater harmony and spirit. My mind demands to think of you as my body breathes for only you. I no longer control the simple task of exhaling. Your love allows me to survive. A solemn passion is conceived in my heart, it leans to you, draws you to my center and springs to life, wrapping my existence around you. I do not easily surrender my heart, yet it has been yours from the beginning. The first time you hold me in your arms I'll feel a longing to linger a moment and a lifetime in that soft, sensual tenderness I'll find in you. I won't be able to defend my heart from you.

You have become a necessity in my life, and I know that I love you. I will love our private world, free of limitations and full of expectations. Our place where we can express emotions so full of life they burst into a million stars lighting up the heavens where love is born. You will always be able to take me to that place and I will always cherish it. When your eyes meet mine, it will be as if your soul enters mine. I cannot wait for the time when, finally, in my sleep I can reach for you. I'll find you near and submit myself to my dreams knowing your love will be there in the morning. I have yet to experience such a beautiful and flawless happiness as this love you will give to me. You'll overwhelm me and exhaust me at the same time. I'll be so much in love with you.

Forever Always,
Your True Love

Section One
The Forbidden One

"She let it go. She is ready to vibrate higher and become a magnet to miracles. Now she is in this place where everything feels right. Her heart is calm. Her soul is lit. Her vision is clear. She's at peace with where she's been… and at peace with where she's headed."

The Chase

A chase is what I desire!

When she walks away uncertain
She wants you to understand.

When she turns her back to you in bed
She needs your warm embrace.

When she tells you, you're the only one
She is expecting confirmation.

When she gives up her world, just to be in yours
She is longing for a commitment.

Every woman wants and needs to feel that they are
desired. We need to feel that we are loved.

Your woman desires your chase.

Love Unimagined

Sometimes when you're married
You drift away within.
Outside you stroll together
Inside you live in sin.

A rich imagination
Provides your ecstasy
A cordless, mobile heaven
Where everything is free.

The garden that you tend
Is not the one you roam
The part of you that sings
Is not the one at home.

A strange and burning life
What's real is not what's true
And no one knows the passion
That you know is inside of you.

And so, you are distracted
Two people in a jar
Bound by love and fate
Yet never what you are

Until by chance life rips
A hole right through your wall
And nothing you've imagined
Looks like love at all.

You, instead...

If I had married you instead of him
I would not be burning with regret
Trapped by years, choked by dreams strangled by reality
My hopes before my life turned dim.

I would not now be burning with regret
For having married for lust instead of love.
My hopes before my life turned dim
I now live but in the darkness of where you were.

For having married more for lust instead of love
I'm punished with a husband whom I despise.
I live but in the darkness of where you were
My hopes are the harvest of your haunting eyes.

I'm punished with a husband whom I despise
Trapped by years, choked by dreams, strangled by reality
My hopes.... The harvest of your haunting eyes.
If I had married you instead of him.

Please Don't Ask

A passionate affair shadows your every thoughtful glee
I pass by and you fill your eyes with every sight of me
My feminine physique, my touch leaves you breathless
I kiss you all over and you magically fall into pieces.

You breathe in my scent and you yearn for more
I lean back and you scream the name you adore
With every gentle caress, to each stroke of delight
I burn for you and you are loved, but only for the night.

As flesh on flesh celebrate and free our desires
The waters needed to cool down our lustful fires
And as I lay on my back, I ask only from the start
Please don't fall in love, don't ask for my heart.

You cannot ask for something I cannot give
You're handsome, you're free, teach yourself to live
Don't be like others, explore the world and find your call,
My hope is she'll find you, and you'll know when you fall.

Amazing Chemistry

Never have I felt this way
An intensity that grows with each day
I look into your eyes and something takes over
It's a feeling created by no other
I hear your voice and my heart skips a beat
And I am so thankful we were able to meet
You tell me that the feeling is mutual
But we both know my situation is critical
We are each other's definition of perfect
And now we must take the time to reflect
What should we do?
How could you work?
Could it really be......?
That between us, we share an amazing chemistry

Never Had I Fallen

Your lips speak soft sweetness
Your touch a cool caress
I am lost in your magic
My heart beats within your chest.

I think of you each morning
And dream of you each night
I think of your arms being around me
And cannot express my delight.

Never have I fallen
But I am quickly on my way
You hold a heart in your hands
That has never before been given away.

Simply You

I sometimes feel my heart will burst
From wanting you so much
I can't explain in words of how
I long for your touch.

There is no way I can convey
This emptiness inside
That seems to tear my soul to shreds
As time flies swiftly by.

If I could merely hold you near
For just a little while
If I could simply talk with you
Or only see you smile.

To have you look into my eyes
I want to hear you say
Something that would help
Take all the pain away.

If I have to wait forever
I guess that's what I'll do
For me it will be worth it
To finally be with you...

Sweet Dreams

Every night when I close my eyes
I drift to sweet dreams of you...
I imagine the taste of your lips,
The feel of your hands caressing me,
And the sound of your heart beating to
The same rhythm of mine...

And suddenly I'm strong yet weak
From my need for you...
And when you hold me close,
You look into my eyes as you whisper
How much you love me, I'm carried
Gently to the clouds of your love...

Your love makes me feel so alive and
Proud to be the person I am when I'm with you...
Yet when the stars fade as dawn breaks,
You kiss me goodnight at the door,
And I awake needing you
Even more than I did the day before.

I'm missing you so bad and I wish you were here.
Even though you're far away,
In my heart you will always stay.
I'll never quit wishing you were here by my side,

But until that day, I've only dream about you,
And I escape to that place in my heat,
Where we're never apart.

Risking Pain

The chance of happiness equals the risk of pain
Whenever you love, its too good to be true
Even so, its truer than you believe
Nor will you know till it vanishes again
Time is a sea which opens where you cleave
Yet rolls over what you leave behind.

For now, my love sings in the stars
Or hisses against rocks like the sea
Unraveling your life when you pause to grieve
Returning with the sunlight and with the rain.

Afraid, Yet I Love You...

I am afraid to love, and yet I love you
My fear is like a wall I walked right through
The wall is there, and yet it doesn't stop me
I need it still, and yet I still need you.

I know someday we will be in a field
Surrounded by the blessings of the sky
I'll dance with all the freedom of pure joy
Needing you without a reason why.

I'm still afraid that I might lose my one true love
You might not understand what I'm going through
I long for your time, your touch, and your kiss
Oh, how I'm so afraid to love, yet I love you.

I'll Be There

Although we have to be apart,
We'll always be together
Close enough in my mind and heart
To manage any weather.

Reality is often bleak
But love remains inside
A glass house on a mountain peak
The spring garden surround the outside.

Love can build its own four walls
And heat its own small room
Through icy winds or a blinding forest
Love can be in full bloom.

Though continents drift far downstream
And mountains disappear
Life dissolve into a dream
Our love will still be here...

You'll turn, and I'll be there.

My Cherished Place

I don't mind having no estate to call my own
Mansions of gold and of great luxury
Knowing it's me your heart holds and keeps
Makes me feel a majesty of a thousand folds.

Precious gems and earthly possessions I don't have
Neither do I wish having them to enjoy life
Nothing there could ever match my place
That special place that I cherish.

Both of us are near yet can't reach each other
Bounded by restrictions I wish to conquer
Pain and longings to my hearts these bring
Making both you and I endure great suffering.

Situations like this is really a great trial
Eyes conversing as lips make denial
No matter how we try to hide our feelings
Silent words just came out and they're so revealing.

Is self-sacrifice what we should do?
It's either we hold on to each other or let it go
But, to go on loving each other is a complete taboo
For I belong to him and, she belongs to you.

I rather hurt myself in silence full of pain
Then to feel a sense of unhappiness in this space
One reason this space needs not to be explained
For your heart has been my cherished place.

You and I

You and I are connected
in a way that goes beyond romance,
beyond friendship,
beyond what we've ever had before.
It has defied time, distance,
and changes in ourselves
and in our lives.
It has defied every explanation.
Except one: Pure and simple, we're soulmates.

I can't explain it, I just feel it.
It's there in the way my spirits lift
whenever we talk
The sound of your voice brings me home,
in a way I can't explain
It's in the delight I feel when we laugh
at exactly the same things.
When I'm with you
it's like a tiny place of the universe
shifts into place.
A place it's supposed to be
and all is right with the world.

These things and so many more,
have made me understand
that this is a once in a lifetime
forever connection.
A connection that could only exist
between you and me.

And deep in my soul
I know that our relationship is a rare gift.
One that brings us extraordinary happiness
all through our lives.

Every Time I Look at The Stars

I gazed in your eyes
Such a beautiful view
My heart whispered to me
And that's when I knew
The waves had ceased crashing
On the sand at our feet
Time had stopped passing
His search was complete
I finally discovered
What I'd known all along
A mystery uncovered
That just couldn't be wrong
It was our first kiss
And the day we met
That I realized something
I will never forget
With the stars shining bright

From high up above
Our one word is love.
I knew then these feelings
For my friend were true
The man of my dreams
And my person is you.
I think of it every time

Memoirs of Her Past Loves

That I look at the stars
This memory is mine
But that moment was OURS.

Something Else

Lovers, I've had many
That's forgotten me completely
I've always kept my love true
But its something else with you.

Every touch is like a fiery knife
Ready to destroy my life
Every kiss is soothing glee
That reaches every part of me.

The days of adoring are over
When a start of new flame uncovers
The sinful pleasure and passion
My foolish heart's uncontrolled emotion.

There's something else that shows
Though you may never really know
The rain may wash it all away
But it doesn't get easier with each day.

Unsure of what our future may be
A part of me is yours exclusively
We can't resist, bound, and enslaved
From lustful thoughts, missed and craved.

Its something else, if not true love
It's something else we both can't have
Since you're with her, and I'm with him
We've borrowed time, our secret's within.

Secret Lover

Come into my heart
Fill it with the warm essence of your love
Brighten my day with your sunny smile
And fill my nights with unforgiven passion.
Lay with me under the glowing skies
Whispering sweet nothings in my ear
Those beautiful words of love
That only we would understand
Gently caress my awaiting body
With deliberate and exploring hands
And cover my mouth with passionate kisses
That draw the very soul from my body.
I live to be near you
To feel your gentleness
my world begins and ends in your arms
You intentionally give me unbelievable joy
My heart, my mysteriously secret lover.

My Choice

I've been through so much pain
Strength and passion are what I've gain
Just knowing him, has set my heart free
Now I'm who I've always wanted to be.

I'm no longer afraid to love you
For this is what my heart longs to do
I've never been in love before
It is him whom my heart adores.

My situation is extremely complicated you'll see
"True Love" only happens to others, not me.
I've made vows to someone else, not him
My life is full of pain, my way seems dim.

I didn't know him when the vows were said
If I did I don't think they would have been read
I feel fulfilled knowing he's in my life
My heart no longer feels the stabbing of a knife.

He's loved me passed my pain and sorrow
His love gives me hope for tomorrow
I'm not trying to replace my past with my future
And I want my leaving to be neutral.

I never meant to hurt anyone
But the feelings I had are so far gone
I love him and this is where I want to be
I'm so happy with my choice, 'cause he also chose me!

Haunted Dreams

The mind will make you go crazy
Even though what you dream isn't real
The thought of knowing that it could be
Make it seem like a done deal.

We dream dreams of laughter and happiness
But it's those that we have every now and then
Those that we don't know how to tell
'Cause they're mixed with today and way back when.

When I was a little girl
the dreams that seemed so real that made me sad
has come back to haunt me
and now I'm really mad.

Mad because he's not the same kind
The kind I dealt with before
He would never hurt me like that
Nor would he throw me out the door!

I wish I could just forget about
The past that haunts me all day and night
So that I can love him without boundaries
With my heart and soul.... with all my might.

Section Two
The "First" True One

❧◦❧◦❧◦❧◦❧◦❧◦❧◦❧◦❧◦❧

Your first love isn't always the first person you kiss, or the first person you date…. or even the first person you marry. Your first love is the person you will always compare everyone to. The person that you will never truly get over, even when you've convinced yourself you've moved on. That person who after experiencing love with them, has changed your life in a way that you will never see the world as you saw it before them. You basically have to reintroduce yourself to a whole new world.

Love is unpredictable... and you make that statement so true in every meaning of the word unpredictable. You are my light when all I see is darkness, you are my air when I feel out of breath. My soul would be lost without you, my body yearns for your touch and my heart longs to love only you. Your smile has its way of letting me know that you are content, your eyes lets me know that you love me, your touch... ooo wee... that touch reminds me of how sweet and deep your love is. And when you hold me in your arms, I am confident that it's true love. To be clear on how I feel about you, know that the love I have for you reaches to the highest of mountains, flows to the lowest of valleys, and if a light could shine in its place, the whole world would be gleaming. Our love gives me strength to shield away any perpetrators...

It's pure and genuine.

The Feeling

Until we met I didn't know
how light a heart could be
how chained to one by bonds of love
I still could feel so free.

I didn't realize that my dreams
could ever be so real
or when I had all I could want
exactly how I would feel.

This year of love has helped me
through a long-awaited door
where angles parked along our skies
and I could not love you more.

Desire a Lover

Last night, today, tonight I've thought of you
Your fear of loving me, your fear of pain
My own reluctance soon to love again
And why we often flee what we pursue.
I've thought if we could make time disappear
Then we could love with nether hope nor fear.
But when we pause to watch the moment flow
Beneath we see eternity and space
Removing us from all we love and know.
I cannot but anticipate the end...
Desire a lover, yet never lose a friend.

You Are Him... My Lover, My Friend

The Lord has sent you my way...

From the first time we kissed, I knew you were him
The man who captured my heart my world's no longer dim.
You turned my gray skies blue from the moment I laid
eyes on you. I found myself when the Lord placed you in
my view, and that was something only your love could do.
You inspire me to be a better person to this world. The
power in your embrace set no limits for this eagle to soar.

Your love is like fine wine, it gets better with time.
You came into my life when my world was crumbling down.
God made true to his promise, He showed up and showed
out! Because of you I have so much more than I'd ever
dreamed. It looks like we don't have much, but nothing is
what it seems.

With you I have it all...

You are one of my greatest blessings, even if it seems so
small. Today I return with your rib from which God made
me. Your heart can rejoice, now you can love freely. We
stand here presented as one. So, it was said... also
written... AND NOW IT IS DONE!

***Loving you is my heart's desire!!!

Hoping

I was sort of hoping
That you would come along,
Like the answer to my prayer
And the music to my song.

Like the kind of thing that happens
At a special place and time
That will change our lives forever
Like a fantasy of mine.

The fantasy was there before
I ever knew your name
And now that I have found you
We will never be the same.

So, excuse me if I look at you
Forgive me if I stare
At the fantasy I knew before
I saw you standing there.

For I was always hoping
That you would come along
Like the answer to my prayer
And the music to my song.

Constant Thunder in My Soul

I was once lost in darkness, a wandering crazed fool
Teetering on the edge of reason about to plunge into the
depression.

Then a light shone down, lifted me out of darkness
Touched my soul with grace and beat love into my heart.

That was when I met you.

For so long now you have continued to save me, day after
day, you gave me the reason to be, to live and to feel love,
to go on and find my dreams.

I just wanted to let you know that I could never fully
express how much I feel for you, when you love seems so
simple, how could you put into words the power of desire
I have for you.

My heart beats because of you, my soul is bright and
alive, because of you. And even when the trials of today
seem to distract me, my love is always devoted to you, it
is eternal within my heart...

Like a constant thunder in my soul.

When I consider what you've done for me...

You've freed the love in my heart...
and I've never been so happy.
You took my heart's broken pieces
and made it whole.
The love you give has touched my soul.

I see what you are to me...
I believe this is real, I must be in love!!!

My mind, body, and soul say... Thank you!

I'm Happy

I am happy when I'm remembering his touch sending my body into shock as my mind opens to the essence of True Love.

I am happier when I'm next to him listening to his every heartbeat as he holds me so gently.

I am happiest when I'm looking into his eyes staring at his very soul as his heart captures mines "oh so" quietly.

My Song

You taught me how to laugh again,
and gave me back my smile,
Restored my faith in people
when everyone seemed vile.

You were as if the sun came up
on my darkest night,
And bade the blackness
rustling up some joyful morning light.

And inexplicably my heart rose up
and twirled me round
So sudden in its expert art
scarcely touched the ground.

With you I am filled with light
and all my feelings dance
You are my song, my wings, my flight,
my truth, and my romance.

Time

Sometimes time cracks open like a nut
Revealing life's meat neatly nestled in.
Between such moments, time is like a river
Flowing towards some dark and angry dream.

My love for you breaks through the skin of sky,
Breaks through the dream of time, more real

I choose to anchor life on this fixed point,
A passion deep enough to plumb the sea.

Did this love choose me when we first met?
Or was I seized by something more than life?
All I know is through our love I've found
A loveliness more tangible than time.

All The Reasons

From the touch of your hands and the sweet romance
You make me quiver.

From the sound of your voice when you say "I love you"
You make me shiver.

From the way you feel, "Oh so good" that sends me in a
state of awe
Your love is kind.

From that "oh so sexy" look that makes me weak
I'm so glad you're mine.

My heart and soul are overjoyed from the love we share
The blessings have overflowed.

Like the light of the moon that illuminates the blackened
skies
You brighten my world.

I'm a prisoner that has a life sentence
The jail is your heart...

Like the warmth of the sun that affects everyone
I'm the luckiest girl!

From the quality time spent to the "true love" we
cherish
Are all the reasons we should never part!

The Little Things

It's the little things in life I pay most attention to
sometimes the smallest insult can hurt the most
A little white lie can ruin everything.

It's the little things in life I cherish most. One flower
stands out in a garden of hundreds. Two kids pointing at
the night sky not sure what they're thinking but they
too, appreciate the little things.

It's the little things in life you do for me that I love. A
quick touch of your hand as we walk past one another. A
little but tight hug holding me up when I want to fall.

One thing I adore most the way you look at me, a little
turn of the head while I stare into your eyes you look into
my heart.

It's the little things that have me falling for you
It's the little that kept me in love with you...
And it will be the little things that will keep me loving
you!

You Are My Sunshine

You are everything I ever wanted

On you my future happiness depends

Unless I'm with you, all my thoughts are haunted

After seeing you, my anxiety ends

Reason warns me that I am in danger

Eventually, everything must fade

My love, like yours, is flammable in anger

Yet my trust is such, I'm not afraid

Something in our love's more than emotion

Underneath each thought and each desire

Not even all the water in the ocean

Seems up to putting out this one small fire

How could this be? Within our love is something

Immeasurable, infinite, and good

Nothing in all life can match this one thing

Each other passion would be if it could.

With You

When I'm with you, eternity is a step away
My love continues to grow with each passing day.

This treasure of love, I cherish within my soul
How much I love you... you'll never really know.

You bring a joy to my heart, I've never felt before
With every touch of your hand, I love you more.

Whenever we say goodbye, whenever we part
Know I hold your love deep inside my heart.

So, these seven words I pray you hold true, "I will love
you, Always and Forever!" For you are the one who makes
me whole, you've captured my heart and touched my soul.

For you are the one that stepped out of my dreams
Gave me new hope showed me what love means.

For you alone are my reason to live
From the compassion you show to the care you give.

You came into my life and made me complete
Each time I see you my heart skips a beat.

For you define beauty in both body and mind
Your soft, gentle face more beauty I'll never find.

The Heart Knows

You walked lightly into my life
Captivating and loving my mind
At first I never cared who you were
Now I don't know who I am without you
You kissed me I felt the world change,
You held me and I heard my heart awaken
You loved me and my soul was born anew.

Now my heart knows who you are
And with every breath and every step
I take down lonely roads, your hand is my staff
Your voice is my guide, your strength is my shelter.

And all my pain, you took as your own
And all my fears, you cast into the sea
All of my doubt lost in your eyes.

And no matter if you choose to stay or go
My life is forever changed
Just because you loved me for a moment in time and
because I choose to love you for the rest of mine.

In Silence...

Words twist and tumble
Through my mind
But I can't grab the right word
Or the right line
So, we sit
In silence
But it's not uncomfortable
In face I love it
I rest my head on your chest
As we lay here
Lovers entwined
Hearts tangled
I raised my head
And look into your eyes
I see our love
Almost as if it's a real force
I don't want to lose this moment
I lay my head on your chest again
And now I can feel your heart
My heart skips a beat
And I finally find the words I'm looking for...
"I love you"

Falling In Love With You...

I never thought I'd fall in love with you
I thought someday, of course, I'd fall in love
But what it would feel like, I just never knew
I'd no idea what I was thinking of
And then, somewhere between my need and pleasure
Walking neither overjoyed nor sad,
I looked into my heart and saw a treasure
Worth more than anything I'd ever had.
WOW! This is love! I thought. And then,
I wanted to give my life to see your happiness
Suddenly, from nowhere, I was haunted
Needy, joyful, tearful, glad, obsessed.
My love for you has brought me out of me
The beauty in your heart has set me free.

The Way You Make Me Feel

You make me feel special, you make me feel new
You make me feel loved with everything you do.

You hold me close when I am sad
You wipe the tears from my face.
Every time we are together
It seems like the perfect place.

My eyes light up when you enter a room
I smile when we are together
No matter how bad things are
You always make them better.

I love the way you kiss me
The way you hold me tight.
I love the way you touch me
I could be with you all night.

I love the way you can make me laugh
For absolutely no reason at all
I love how no matter what I do
You will be there to catch me when I fall.

I just want you to know that even though we fight
I will always love you no matter what, day and night.

My Number One

All my life I've waited
Floating, dreaming, wishing
For the day when you would come my way
That day has come
My heart flutters at the sound of your voice
My hands shake as I reach for your touch
In heaven there can only be a better place
Soaring through the clouds
The wind beating at my skin
Breathing heavy, feeling numb
You're all I need, my number one.

Tears stream down my face, burning my eyes
Happy tears, thankful smiles
Knowing I can hold you, embrace you
Fearless of the unknown, content with life
No longer will I feel the sharpened knife
Of hurt, pain and suffering
Misery's no longer my name
You're all I want, you're all I need
Visions of forever on the horizon
Angels have bought you here to me
For reasons clear to see, like diamonds
Sparkling, shining in the days sun
You're all I need, my number one.

My Heaven

It's pure bliss when I'm with you
Just like beginning my life brand new
I look forward to seeing your face
I can't wait to feel your strong embrace
Laughing and talking with you like an old friend
Making love to you over and over again
Looking deep into your dreamy brown eyes
As I gather my thoughts, and hold in my cries
I miss you intensely, I'm close to breaking down
If I indulge myself to cry, I might drown
Being with you is such a beautiful expression
And if loving you is so true, then dreaming of you is my
heaven.

You Bring Me Joy

It's amazing how I feel when I'm around you
How my heart pounds when you come into a room.
I look at you and think: My Love! My Soulmate!
And everything I am is in full bloom.

I feel as though you must be mine,
Not as a possession but a connection
Something almost imaginable
The free devotion of another soul.

As though I were about to enter heaven
Just within the hour condemned to die,
My mind with one fierce thought
Of only you, the reason why.

All of This

You're the thought that starts each morning
The conclusion to each day
You are in all that I do and everything I say.

You're the smile on my face the twinkle in my eye
The warmth inside my heart the fullness in my life.

You're the hand that's laced in mine
And the coat upon my back
My friend, my love, and my shoulder to lean on.

You're my silly, mature, caring,
Thoughtful, bright, and honest guy
The one who holds me tightly when I need to cry.

You're my dimple in my cheek
The ever-constant tingle in my soul.
The voice that makes me weak the happiness in my life.

You are all I've wanted...
You are all I need...
You are all I've dreamed off...
You are all this to me.

Every Second Beat

If I had a thousand pages
I could never name them all
The reasons that I love you
For the list would be too tall.

I love you for the melody
I hear in your voice
The way your dreamy eyes hold me...
A captive, but by choice.

I love you for your gentle hands
That melt away my pain
I love you for your loving heart
That made mine beat again.

I love you for your loving smile
With which my old heart soars
These are some of the reasons
Every second beat is yours.

I Want To Be The One

I want to be the one you see in your dreams
The one that reminds you of what love really means.

I want to be the one that makes you happy inside
The one you run to when all you want to do is hide.

I want to be the one you look for in a crowd
The one you miss when I'm not around.

I want to be the one you show off to your friends
The one you won't leave alone to cry in the end.

I want to be the one who picks you up when you fall
The one you want to talk to, the first one you call.

I want to be the one you look at and say she's the one
The one you think of when night falls and the day is done,

I want to be the one you would drive fifteen hours to see
And you wouldn't mind if you could only stay for three.

I want to be the one you would sing for any day
The one you'll comfort when distress comes my way.

I want to be the one, the only one for you
The one you love to whom you'll always be true.

LOVE, Forever

I love you deeply
I love you so much
I love the sound of your voice
And the way that we touch.
I love your warm smile
And your kind, thoughtful way,
The joy that you bring
To my life every day.
I love you today
As I have from the start
And I'll love you forever
With all my heart.

Because of You

Because of you
My world is now whole

Because of you
Love lives in my soul

Because of you
I have laughter in my eyes

Because of you
I am no longer afraid of goodbyes.

You are my pillar
My stone of strength
With me through seasons
And great times at length.
My love for you is pure
Effortless through space and time
It grows stronger every day
Knowing that you'll always be mine.
And if there ever come a time
When we meet at the alter
I will gladly say "I do!" for I have it all now
...and it's because of you.

THE SCENT OF MY MAN

The smell that sends chills up and down my spine
The smell that is so pleasant, lets me know he's mine

The smell is not worn every day
But I can sniff him out miles away

The smell is so mesmerizing... his touch, tantalizing!

His scent would make me do things I've never done
Like declare my love for him on day one!

I was careful I didn't give into his scent
Until I prayed and confirmed, he was meant.

Meaning God sent him to me
His true love is what He required me to be.

And at the end of the day when it's all said and done
I'll still be in love with the scent of only one.

It's Real

Sometimes at night when I look to the sky
I start thinking of you and then ask myself, why?

Why do I love you? I think and smile
Because I know the list could run on for miles.

The whisper of your voice, the warmth of your touch
So many little things that make me love you so much.

The way you support me and help with my emotions
The way you care and show your devotion.

The way that your kiss fills me with desire
And how you hold me like the warmth of a cozy fire.

The way your eyes shine when you look at me
Lost with you forever is where I want to be.

The way that I feel when you're by my side
A sense of completion and overflowing pride.

The dreams that I dream that all involve you
The possibilities I see and the things we can do.

How you finish the puzzle that's inside my heart
How that deep in my soul you're the most important
part.

I could go on for days telling of what I feel
But all you really must know is that my love for you is
real!

Changed Life

I don't think you will
ever fully understand
how you've touched my life
and made me who I am.

I don't think you could ever know just how truly special
you are that even on the darkest nights you are my
brightest star.

I don't think you will every fully comprehend
How you've made my dreams come true
Or how you've opened my heart
To love and to the wonders it can do.
You've allowed me to experience
something hard to find,
unconditional love that exists
in my body, soul, and mind.

I don't think you could ever feel
All the love I have to give
And I'm sure you'll never realize
You've been my will to live.

59

You are an amazing person
without you I don't know where I'd be
Having you in my life
Fulfils every part of me.

Why I Stopped Dreaming

I used to dream of a strong man
And his loving arms to hold me.
I used to dream of heroic knights
And how gracious they would be.

I used to dream of how I would never settle
For anything less than the best
I used to dream of how he would magically
Lay all my fears at rest.

I used to dream of fairy tales
How wonderful they would be
I used to dream of story books
All patterned after me.

I used to dream of a lot of things
But the moment I met you
I immediately stopped dreaming
Because all of my dreams had come true.

MY KING

I look deep within my man's soul.... I see Power!

Within my man dwell those slumbering powers, those powers that because of the woman he has by his side would astonish him. Powers he never dreamed of until the day I came into his life. Powerful forces that have revolutionized his life, and also mine. He possesses this power because he doesn't have to question his position. Although constantly tempted by others he remains true to his heart. Not one could fathom what the two shares. What they have cannot be explained, it just is!

iForever... will cherish what we had!

Section Three
The Lost One

One of the hardest things you will ever have to do is grieve the loss of a true love that is still alive.

I've waited...

We were sleeping under the same star
Dreaming dreams of love
I'm wandering where you are?
Seems like forever that I've waited for you
In a world of disappointments, one thing is true
All I've ever wanted was to find that "one" for me
And in this world of lonely people, I found you
How blessed I am that I found you
Now that you are here... I'm still waiting

Have I Lost You?

Searching for that connection
That one we used to know
I don't know if it's gone away
And just refuses to show.

The feeling of that magical place
That touch, that kiss that made me weak
That sent me head over heels for you
The one that made me reach my peak

What was shared was so special
That once between me and you
I would do anything to get it back
Because without you, its misty blue.

Blue from the pain I feel inside
Not saying it's your fault or anything
My only goal was to make you happy...
...and to see you smile again.

Why?

Why did he stop loving me?
How could he forget so fast?
Does he still feel love for me?
How could this "true" love not last?

I've learned I can't believe my eyes
Nor trust the instincts of my heart
I look upon a sea of lies
Too wide to cross, too deep to chart.

And yet I am condemned to sail
Upon that sea that's washed in pain
Love hides its truth behind a veil
That none may know they love in vain.

You say you want to be just friends
But does mean goodbye?
Is that the easy way to end
The wish without the why?

There's something lovely like a song
That's waiting to be heard
Or like the feelings that belong
To some unspoken word.

I cannot simply smile and stay calm
And stay within the confines of this booth
I'd rather take the risk of asking frankly
For the untold truth.

You Say You Need Space...

Although you say you need space
I want to have my say
Without invading your domain
Or forcing you away.

I respect the choice you made
And all that you decide
It hurts like hell
I feel like something inside of me died.

As a lake deep in the woods
Awaits a cool fresh breeze
My heart will harden
While you do as you please.

How Do I Go On?

We went too far too fast
and yet I don't want this to end
How do I step back from love
and keep you as a friend?

How do I feel affection
and refrain from undue touch?
How do I tell you how I feel
and still not say too much?

I know I led you to expect
far more than I could give
before I have the strength to know
just how I want to live.

The fault is mine,
and I now must ask of you
Forgiveness and the simple space
to do what you must do.

Please don't pull away from me
in anger or in pain
for in our mutual respect
we both have much to gain.

Memoirs of Her Past Loves

Section Four
The Extras

"You glow different when a real man is taking care of your heart"

"Based on a psychologic study, a crush only lasts four months. If it exceeds that then you are already in love."

Light, My Beauty

He was a meteor that hit my life
I didn't even see coming.

He blew up my world and all of my plans.

He unearthed the truth in me... Made me take off this
mask I've been wearing.

So that he could see the light in me...
And the world could see the beauty he sees.

I'm in Love with You!

...so much that I can't seem to direct my mind to NOT think of you. The mind and heart want what it wants, and I have no control over them anymore.

For this reason and so many more, I love you!

It is you that my heart yearns for
It is you that my mind won't let go
It is you that my body feens for
It is you, and only you that my soul already knows!

Lonely...

...the feeling you get when you're missing the one you love.

I'm lonely.... The feeling I feel when you're not here with me when I need you most.

I'm not needy, yet I need you!

Nights turn into days because I don't sleep.
Thoughts of you have taken over my mind.
You've come into my life and invaded the space in my heart that was protected and hidden from the outside world.

I don't know how this happened, but somehow you made your way in.

Craving You

I need you to come close to me, not in a physical perspective that allows you to keep away...

Let's get deep into the pain of forgotten passions wrapped in the tenderness of our souls.

Let's fly into our endless thoughts and emotions until we find out landing spot...

I know you can get into me if I allow it... and to my surprise your eyes are wide open, but not because my legs have been opened.

Let this moment simply be exactly what we desire it to be. Unbridled energy flowing back and forth until we have passed out from exhaustion.

Yeah that's it!

I Love You

Love will have you step out of your comfort zone to sacrifice and compromise...

I love you mean that I accept you for the person you are and that I do not wish to change you into someone else.

It means that I do not expect perfection from you.

It means that I love you and will stand by you even through the worst of times.

It means loving you when you're in a bad mood or too tired to do things I want to do.

It means loving you when you're down and not just when you're fun to be around and with.

I love you means that I know your deepest and darkest secrets and don't judge you for them.

It means that I care enough to fight for what we have and that I love you enough to not let go.

It means thinking of you, dreaming of you, wanting, and needing you constantly and hoping the feelings are mutual.

Essence of Love

To love someone means that you have the greatest understanding of them. It means that you love them for everything that they are, and you respect them for everything that they are not.

...love does not come with instructions.
...love does not ask if you're ready.

Don't waste the words, but don't hide behind them either.

"I love you" is not a catch phrase, nor is it the key to unlocking a women's legs. It is the term that defines all that is right between you and the person that encourages you to be who you already are.

"I love you" can be the beginning process to the greatest accomplishments the world has witness to or it can be the memory of greatest times past.

It is my belief that love is undying and no matter the obstacle, it is my goal to bathe myself in the "essence of your love."

If I Ever Fall in Love, AGAIN! I Wanna...

...fall in love with someone who wants to know my favorite color and how love my coffee.

...fall in love with someone who loves the way I laugh and would do absolutely anything to hear it.

...fall in love with someone who puts their head on my chest just to hear my heartbeat.

...fall in love with someone who kisses me in public and is proud to show me off to everyone they know.

...fall in love someone who makes me question why I was afraid to fall in love in the first place.

...fall in love with someone who would never ever want to hurt me.

...fall in love with someone who falls in love with my flaws and knows I am perfect just the way I am.

...fall in love with someone who knows that I am the ONE they would love to wake up to the rest of our lives.

I wanna love this journey...

I wanna dance until my knees hurt. I wanna laugh until my belly aches. I wanna stay awake until we doze off in the middle of a sentence because the conversation is just that good. I wanna sleep until the sun wakes us up.

I wanna find out what our song sound like and sing the melody of our love... even if it's off key.

I like when my heart skips a beat...
I like when my stomach turns in knots because you took my breath away by the way you look at me.

I don't wanna miss a moment of this life called love with you. I wanna be at peace knowing the love I'm receiving is genuine. I wanna say "I love talking to you (even in silence), I love walking with you, I love holding your hand, I love this journey and I'm proud. I'm proud of the way you wear your imperfections and most importantly, I'm proud of the way you've decided to love me."

You Are My One

You like someone because of all of the qualities, and you love someone despite their insecurities.

...the way you walk
...the way you talk
...the way you smell

...the way you look at me, in a way that no other man has never looked at me.

...the way you kiss me, it melts my soul.

And your touch...

...the way you touch me, and our bodies are naturally in sync, in a way that lets me know that you need me just as much as I need you.

How amazing it is to find someone who wants to hear all about the little things that goes on in your head!

Love... On His Terms

I've fallen! I stop believing that true love exists and then you show up and changed my mind. You are that living soul that God has for me... that one He's been saving for me?!

...only to find our there is yet another obstacle.

I question myself daily, is this real?

I ask God to reveal who it is He has for me and every time, it's you!

...in the form of an "out of the blue" phone call or just something "around the way" that would remind me of your presence in my life.

It's crazy because you belong to someone else.

...why am I head over heels about you?
...why am I sooooo in love with you?
...why can't I walk away?

I've been praying for my own. And in my mind, you are! And the fact of the matter is... I can't stop loving you. But what's scary is that I don't want to!

Check out my website to view my current
and upcoming books.

www.Dunlap7.com

Follow me on my social media pages below
to connect and interact with me.

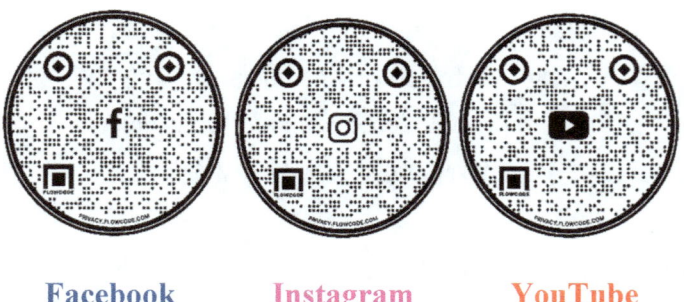

Facebook   Instagram   YouTube

When Yvonne a.k.a. Sapphire started writing, she wrote poetry and short stories. She produced her first project in 2010, when she created a picture/poem book for the love of her life at the time. She never thought to publish any of her poems until she decided that it was time for her to release her thoughts and free her mind of the connections she once shared. This publication is a collection of some of her poems from her past experiences with love.

She is the author of The Woman She Became – Part I and The Woman She Became – Part II. Her books can be found on Amazon and on her website at www.Dunlap7.com.

Sapphire currently lives in Upper Marlboro, MD.